Morris
the Mouse Hunter

Collins
YELLOW
STORYBOOK

*Also by Vivian French
and Guy Parker-Rees*

MORRIS IN THE APPLE TREE

Morris
the Mouse Hunter

by Vivian French

illustrated by Guy Parker-Rees

CollinsChildren'sBooks

An imprint of HarperCollinsPublishers

First published in Great Britain by
CollinsChildren'sBooks 1995

1 3 5 7 9 10 8 6 4 2

CollinsChildren'sBooks is a division of
HarperCollins Publishers Ltd.,
77-85 Fulham Palace Road,
Hammersmith, London W6 8JB

Text copyright © Vivian French 1995
Illustrations copyright © Guy Parker-Rees 1995

The author and illustrator assert the moral right
to be identified as the author/illustrator of the work.

Printed and bound in Great Britain
by HarperCollins Manufacturing Ltd, Glasgow

0 00 674895 3

For Bonnie,
a cat with great charm
like her owner, Fiona

Morris the Mouse Hunter

Morris was ginger and white, and very fat.

"Morris," said his mother, "you're much too fat."

"That's right," said his big sister Rose. "What you need is exercise."

"Exercise?" said Morris. "What's that?"

His mother looked at him.

"Running and jumping," she said.

"And bouncing and pouncing,"
said his little brother Tom. He
bounced up and down. "Like me!"

"Oh," said Morris. He licked his paw. "I'm very good at licking and purring," he said. "And I'm EVER so good at eating."

"We know," said his mother.
"But now it's time for running and
jumping."

"Must I?" said Morris.
"Yes," said his mother.

Morris began by running. He ran to his food bowl, and he ate up every little scrap.

"I've done my running," he said.
"Can I have a rest?"

"No," said his mother. "You must
do some jumping first."

Morris sighed. "All right," he said, and he jumped on to the large cosy chair in the kitchen. Then he curled up and went to sleep.

"Morris, Morris! Wake up!"

Morris woke up. Rose was pulling
his tail.

"Come along," she said. "It's time for your exercise. You haven't done any bouncing and pouncing."

"Must I?" said Morris.

"Yes," said Rose.

Morris bounced up to his food
bowl, but it was empty.

"I can't bounce any more," he
said. "I'm too hungry."
His mother shook her head. "It's
not time for dinner yet," she said.

"You've got to pounce like me,"
said Tom. He pounced on Morris's
paws, and he pounced on Morris's
tail. "Like that," he said.

"Then can I have my dinner?"
Morris asked.
"We'll see," said his mother.

Morris found a fly buzzing at the window, and pounced. The fly buzzed away, and Morris sat down.

"I'm tired," he said.
"Come along," said his mother, "I want to see you pouncing."

"I've pounced," said Morris. "It buzzed off. Can I have my dinner now?"

"No," said his mother. "One run and one jump and one bounce and one pounce isn't enough." She scratched her ears. "What do you think, Rose?"
Rose stroked her whiskers.

"I know," she said. "Morris can go and catch a mouse."
Morris stared. "A MOUSE?"
"Yes," said Rose.

Morris began to cry. "You said I
could have my dinner if I
pounced," he sobbed, "and I did. I
pounced on a fly. Why can't I have
my dinner? It's not fair."

His mother jumped up on to the large cosy chair.

"You need exercise," she said. "You go and find a mouse, and be sure to run and jump and bounce and pounce. Then you can have your dinner." And she curled up and went to sleep.

Rose began to wash Tom's ears.
"Hurry up, Morris," she said.
"You'll never catch a mouse if you
sit and cry."

Morris walked slowly out of the
kitchen.

He went slowly up the stairs to the
bedroom and into the bathroom.
There was no sign of a mouse.

He came slowly down the stairs
and into the sitting room, but there
was no mouse there either.

"Where can I find a mouse?" he
said to himself. "Everyone is very
mean. All I want is my dinner."

"Morris!" said Rose. Morris jumped.
"Morris, are you looking for a
mouse?"
Morris nodded.

"Good," said Rose. "Mind you sit
very still."
Morris nodded again. He sat down
and licked his paw.
There was a little noise in the
corner of the room. Morris stopped
licking his paw and looked up.
"What's that?" he said.

"Ssssh!" said Rose. "You mustn't say, 'What's that?' You must crouch down and watch and listen."

"Oh," said Morris. "All right." He crouched down and watched and listened. Nothing happened.

Morris sat up again and looked at his paws.

"Bother," he said. "I can't remember which one I've licked. Perhaps I'd better start again."

There was another little noise. A little scratching noise. Morris licked his paws.

"Morris!" said Rose. "What did I tell you?"

"Oh yes," said Morris, and he crouched down. The noise went on scratching. Morris went on watching and listening.
After two minutes Morris was bored.

"What do I do now?" he asked in a loud voice.

"SSSSH!" said Rose. She was crouching down beside Morris, and her eyes were gleaming. Morris yawned.
"BE QUIET!" hissed Rose.
Morris was.

From under the book shelves in
the corner of the room crept a
small grey mouse. Morris stared at
it. The mouse crept a little closer.

"NOW!" said Rose.

"Now what?" asked Morris.

"MERRROW!" said Rose, and she sprang at the mouse. The mouse slid away under Morris's nose and out of the door. Rose sprang after it and Morris heard them rushing through the kitchen.

"Well, well," said Morris.

There was another little scratching
noise. Morris looked up and saw
another mouse tiptoeing out. A
small fat mouse, with drooping
whiskers. She stopped when she
saw Morris, and her nose trembled.

"Hello," said Morris.

"Eek!" said the mouse.

Morris scratched his ears.

"Aren't you going to jump and
pounce at me?" the mouse asked.

"Do you want me to?" said Morris.

"Not really," said the mouse. "But my mother says that's what cats do. She says cats run and jump and bounce and pounce, and mice run away. That's how mice stay

thin, my mother says. They run and run." The mouse sighed. "My mother says I can't have my dinner until I've done some running."

Morris sat up. "Really?" he said.
"Me too. I can't have my dinner
until I've caught a mouse."

The mouse and Morris looked at
each other. Morris shook his head.

"I don't want to catch you," he said.
"I don't want to run and run," said
the mouse.

Morris stroked his whiskers. "So
what shall we do?"
The mouse coughed. "You've got
very nice whiskers," she said.

Morris began to purr.
"If I had a cat's whisker," the
mouse said, "my mother might
think I had run and run."

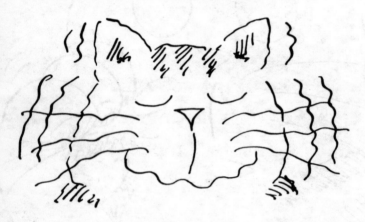

Morris stopped purring. "But that
would hurt," he said.

"You can have one of my
whiskers," the mouse said.
"Then your mother might think
you had run and jumped and
bounced and pounced on me."

"Hurrah!" said Morris.

Morris and the mouse each pulled
out a whisker.
"OW!" said the mouse.

"OW!" said Morris.

The mouse tucked Morris's
whisker under her arm. "Thank
you very much," she said. "I hope
you get your dinner now."

"Thank YOU," said Morris. He
looked at the mouse. "If ever you
want to share my dinner," he said,
"you'd be most welcome."
"I'll remember that," said the
mouse, and she smiled.

"MERRROW!" said Rose and Tom and Morris's mother from the doorway.

"EEEEK" said the mouse's mother
from under the table.

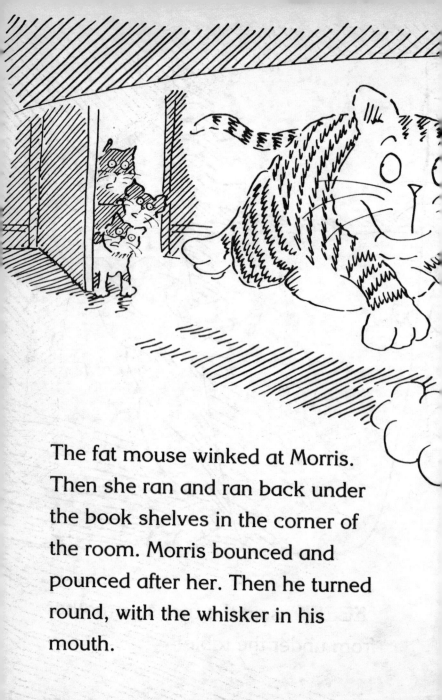

The fat mouse winked at Morris.
Then she ran and ran back under
the book shelves in the corner of
the room. Morris bounced and
pounced after her. Then he turned
round, with the whisker in his
mouth.

"WOW!" said Tom.

"WELL DONE,
MORRIS!"
said Rose.

"GOOD BOY, MORRIS!"
said his mother.

Morris purred. He thought he
heard the mouse's mother saying,
"GOOD GIRL!" from under the
book shelves in the corner, and he
purred louder.

"I think," said Morris's mother,
"that it's time for dinner!"
Morris ran and jumped and
bounced and pounced all the way
to his dinner bowl.